The Elson Readers

Primer

(Revised Edition of Elson-Runkel Primer)

by

William H. Elson
AUTHOR OF GOOD ENGLISH SERIES

AND

Lura E. Runkel
PRINCIPAL, HOWE SCHOOL, SUPERIOR, WISCONSIN

PUBLISHER'S NOTE

Recognizing the need to return to more traditional principles in education, Lost Classics Book Company is republishing forgotten late 19th and early 20th century literature and textbooks to aid parents in the education of their children.

This edition of *The Elson Readers—Primer* was reprinted from the 1920 copyright edition. The text has been updated and edited only where necessary.

We have included a word list of 192 terms at the end of the book with page references to the pages upon which they are used.

The Elson Readers—Primer has been assigned a reading level of 90L. More information concerning this reading level ™ assessment may be attained by visiting www.lexile.com.

© Copyright 2005
Lost Classics Book Company

Library of Congress Catalog Card Number: 2005928901
ISBN 978-1-890623-14-2

Part of
The Elson Readers
Nine Volumes: *Primer* through *Book Eight*
ISBN 978-1-890623-23-4

WILLIAM H. ELSON

In the early 1930s, William Harris Elson capped off a successful career as an educator and author of textbook readers by creating the "Fun with Dick and Jane" pre-primer readers with co-author William Scott Gray. Dick and Jane, their families, friends, and pets entered the popular culture as symbols of childhood, and the books themselves became synonymous with the first steps in learning to read.

In 1909 *The Elson Grammar School Reader*, the first in a nine-volume series of school readers, appeared to immediate success. *The Elson Readers*, which Lost Classics Book Company is reprinting, were among Elson's earliest creations and go well beyond the scope of the "Dick and Jane" books. Following a carefully planned model that stresses both improving comprehension and developing appreciation for literature, Elson organized the books in a way that built on the understanding and skills taught in earlier volumes.

Assisting Elson on the series were publishing house writers Lura Runkel and Christine Keck. Runkel helped on the primer and the first and second volume, while Keck worked on the fifth through the eighth volume. Obviously both writers were schooled well in Elson's methodology, as the series displays remarkable consistency and accuracy throughout the entire set of books.

Through the eighth grade, or age 13 to 14, each succeeding book in the *Elson Readers* series introduces students to increasingly complex genres and better writers. The result of using the series as intended is better reading skills and comprehension, as well as a growing appreciation for good writing. But the books are so thorough that they may be used individually and still advance a student's understanding and appreciation for the types of writing in a particular volume.

3

Born on November 22, 1854, in Carroll County, Ohio, Elson lived through a tumultuous period, becoming an educator who helped usher in numerous innovations. Although he did not receive his A.B. degree from Indiana University until 1895, he was active as a schoolteacher and as a school administrator for many years before, beginning with his first teaching assignment in 1881. By 1907 he had established the first technical high school in the nation in Cleveland, Ohio, where he served as school superintendent from 1906-12.

Elson's contributions to teaching children to read and appreciate literature included not only the *Elson Readers* but many other series for which he served as primary author or editor, including *Good English* (3 vols., 1916); *Child-Library Readers* (9 vols., 1923-34); and *Elson Junior Literature* (2 vols., 1932). By the time of his death on February 2, 1935, his books had sold over fifty million copies and were in use in 34 countries on every continent.

Besides helping to create the engaging "Fun with Dick and Jane" books, William Harris Elson implemented a developmental approach to learning reading skills that still works extremely well. Lost Classics Book Company's republication of this volume from the *Elson Readers* provides access to a book that will provide children with a delightful and effective learning experience.

David E. Vancil, Ph.D.
Indiana State University

Biographical Dictionary of American Educators. 3 Vols. Edited by John F. Ohles. Westport, CT: Greenwood Press, 1978. Alphabetical entry.

The National Cyclopaedia of American Biography. Volume 26. New York: James T. White & Co., 1937. pp. 367-68.

Contents

5

INTRODUCTION

This book is based upon the belief that interesting material is the most important factor in learning to read, that the keynote of interest is the story-plot, and that the child's delight in the oral story should be utilized in the very *first steps* of reading. This basis is the distinguishing feature of the *Primer*.

In consequence, *real stories*, rich in dramatic action, have been chosen—stories which make use of the child's curiosity in "what is going to happen next"—stories which have a plot, a series of incidents, and an outcome. The story element has been unfolded in such a way as to make *each page a distinct unit*. The *Primer* lessons presuppose that the teacher has first told the children the fuller stories, as given in the *Teacher's Guide*. While these oral stories will add greatly to the children's content and interest, nevertheless, the stories in the *Primer* are complete units in themselves. "Review Stories," systematically introduced, refresh the child's memory of words found in previous lessons.

The sources of children's literature have been searched for stories of genuine interest, which deal with life within the range of the child's experience. The stories and verses chosen—thirty in all—make a strong appeal to children by reason of their conceits and their joyous note. Moreover, these stories impress a wholesome influence of high ethical ideals, particularly the ideal of *service to others*. During World War One, American children gained a new conception of this ideal, and this book lays the foundation for perpetuating the lesson through a large number of its stories, notably, "The White Dove," "Bobbie and the Apples," "Alice and Her Mother," "The Windmill," "How Patty Gave Thanks," "The Little Christmas Tree," "In the Barnyard," and "Alice and the Bird." Modern stories by such well-known writers of children's literature as Laura E. Richards, Maud Lindsay, Emilie Poulsson, Carolyn S. Bailey, and others are included, as well as some of the simplest and best of the Mother Goose rhymes and folk tales.

7

ANIMALS AND BIRDS

THE CAT'S DINNER

Alice said, "Come, cat.
Come to dinner."
The cat said, "No.
We will find a dinner."

9

The cat saw a bird.

The kittens saw it, too.

The bird saw the cat.

It saw the kittens, too.

The bird flew away.

The cat said, "Come kittens!
Come to the barn."
The cat went to the barn.
The kittens went, too.
The cat saw a mouse.
The mouse saw the cat.
The mouse ran away.

The cat went to the house
The kittens went, too.
We said, "Come, cat, come!
Come, kittens, come!"
We gave them milk for dinner.

LILLIAN M. ALLEN

SPOT'S KITTENS

Spot is my cat.

She is black and white.

Come, Spot, come!

I like Spot.

Spot likes me.

Spot has four kittens.

One kitten is white.

One kitten is black.

I see a gray kitten, too.

One kitten is like spot.

It is black and white.

One day it rained.

Spot was wet.

The kittens were wet, too.

Spot said, "Mew, mew!

We are wet! We are wet!"

Spot went into the house.

The kittens went, too.

They went to sleep.

JOSEPHINE JARVIS

ALICE AND HER KITTEN

Father said, "Come, Alice.
Come to me.
See the basket.
What is in it?
Can you guess?"

ALICE: What is in the basket?

FATHER: Can you guess?

ALICE: Is it a bird?

FATHER: No, it is not a bird.

ALICE: It is a little dog!

FATHER: No, it is not a dog.

ALICE: Is it a kitten?

FATHER: Yes, it is a kitten.

ALICE: Is it for me?

FATHER: Yes, it is for you.

The kitten is black.

Alice likes her kitten.

She gave it some milk.

The kitten likes milk.

Alice likes milk, too.

The kitten said, "Mew, mew!"

It went to sleep.

JANE L. HOXIE

WHAT WAS IN THE NEST?

The girls saw a nest.

It was a little nest.

It was in a tree.

The girls saw two birds.

Can you see them?

They were pretty birds.

They were in the tree.

Mother bird sat on the nest.

One day she flew from the nest.

What was in the nest?

Can you guess?

The girls saw eggs in the nest.

They saw one, two, three, four eggs.

The four eggs were blue.

Mother bird sat on the nest.

She sat there day after day.

One day she flew from the nest.

She sat in the tree.

She sang and sang.

Father bird sang, too.

The girls looked in the nest.

Can you guess what they saw?

Four little birds were in the nest.

Soon they could fly.

Mother bird said, "Fly, fly!"

Father bird said, "Fly, fly!"

They flew from the nest.

They flew from tree to tree.

One day they flew away.

The girls said, "Good-bye, good-bye!"

THE WHITE DOVE

The dove flew to the barn.

It saw a white cow.

The dove said, "Coo, coo!

See my pretty wings!

Don't you wish you had wings?

You could fly and fly and fly."

The cow said, "Moo, moo!

I give milk to boys and girls.

Moo, moo! I don't want to fly!"

The dove flew to the sheep.

It said, "Coo, coo!

Don't you wish you had wings?

You could fly and fly and fly."

The sheep said, "Baa, baa!

I give wool to boys and girls.

The wool keeps them warm.

Baa, baa! I don't want to fly!"

24

The dove flew to the horse.

It said, "Coo, coo!

Don't you wish you had wings?

You could fly and fly and fly."

The horse said, "No, no!

I give rides to boys and girls.

No, no! I don't want to fly!"

The dove flew to the hen.

It said, "Coo, coo!

Don't you wish you could fly away?"

The hen said, "Cluck, cluck!

I give eggs to boys and girls.

I don't want to fly away."

"Coo, coo!" said the dove.

"Are you all happy?"

The cow said, "Moo, moo! Yes, yes!"

The sheep said, "Baa, baa! Yes, yes!"

The hen said, "Cluck, cluck! Yes, yes!"

The horse said, "Yes, yes!"

The dove said,

    "Coo, coo, coo!

    I am happy, too."

She flew to her nest.

HARRIET WARREN

27

THE JAY AND THE DOVE

Boy: Where do you come from, Mr. Jay?

Jay: From the land of play,
From the land of play.

Boy: Where is that, Mr. Jay?

Jay: Far away. Far away.

Boy: Where do you come from, Mrs. Dove?

Dove: From the land of love,
From the land of love.

Boy: How do you get there, Mrs. Dove?

Dove: Look above. Look above.

L. Alma-Tadema

29

BOBBIE AND THE APPLES

Bobbie was a little boy.

His mother said, "I like apples.

Can you get some for me?"

Bobbie said, "Yes, Mother.

I will go to the apple tree.

I will get some for you.

Good-bye, Mother, good bye."

Bobbie went to the apple tree.

He looked and looked.

He could not see any apples.

He said, "Good morning, apple tree.

Will you give me some apples?"

The apple tree said, "No, Bobbie.

I have no apples for you.

I gave my apples away."

Bobbie saw a cat.

He said, "I want some apples.

I want them for Mother.

Who will give me some?

Can you tell me?"

The cat said, "Mew, mew, mew!

I have no apples for you.

I want milk for dinner.

Mew, mew, mew!"

The cat went to the house.

Bobbie saw a dog.

He said, "Good morning, dog.

I want some apples for Mother.

Who will give me some?

Can you tell me?"

The dog said, "Bow-wow, bow-wow!

Go to the cow.

The cow will tell you."

Bobbie said, "Thank you, dog."

Bobbie ran to the cow.

He said, "Good morning, cow.

I want some apples for Mother.

Who will give me some?

Can you tell me?"

The cow said, "Moo, moo, moo!

I like apples, too.

Go to the farmer.

He has some apples."

Bobbie ran to the farmer.

He said, "Good morning, Mr. Farmer.

Have you some apples?

I want some for Mother."

The farmer said, "Yes, little boy.

I will give you some apples.

Come with me."

They went to the house.

Bobbie saw a bag full of apples.

He said, "May I have three apples?

I want them for Mother."

The farmer said, "Yes, little boy.

You may have four apples.

One apple is for you."

Bobbie said, "Thank you, Mr. Farmer.

I will give three to Mother."

Away he ran to his mother.

Mother said, "What pretty apples!
"Did you bring them all for me?"
Bobbie said, "I have four apples.
Three are for you.
One is for me."
Mother said, "Thank you, Bobbie.
Where did you get them?"
Bobbie said, "I went to the farmer.
The farmer gave them to me."
Mother said, "You are a good boy."

KATE WHITING PATCH—ADAPTED

ALICE AND HER MOTHER

Mother said, "Come, Alice.
Sing little sister to sleep."
Alice said, "I want to play.
I don't want to sing to Sister.
I want to play in the meadow.
The sheep plays there all day.
I want to play all day, too."
Mother said, "You may play all day.
You may go to the meadow."

Alice ran to the meadow.

She saw a sheep there.

Alice said, "Good morning, sheep.

Will you play with me?

We can play all day."

The sheep said, "Baa, baa!

I cannot play all day.

I must get my dinner.

I make wool for Master.

I cannot play all day."

A dog was in the meadow.

Alice ran to the dog.

She said, "Good morning, dog.

Will you play with me?

We can play all day."

The dog said, "Bow-wow!

I cannot play all day.

I must look after the sheep.

I cannot leave them alone.

I cannot play all day."

A cow was in the meadow.

Alice ran to the cow.

She said, "Good morning, cow.

Will you play with me?

We can play all day."

The cow said, "Moo, moo!

I cannot play all day.

I must find my dinner.

I want to find some corn.

I give milk for your dinner.

I cannot play all day."

A horse was in the meadow.

Alice ran to the horse.

She said, "Good morning, horse.

Will you play with me?

We can play all day."

The horse said, "Oh, no!

I cannot play all day.

I give rides to boys and girls.

I take milk to your mother.

I cannot play all day."

Alice said, "I will go home.

No one will play with me."

Soon she came to a bird.

She said, "Good morning, bird.

Will you play with me?

We can play all day."

The bird said, "No, thank you.

I must make my nest.

I cannot play all day."

Alice went home.

She saw her cat there.

She said, "Good morning, Spot.

Will you play with me?

We can play all day."

Spot said, "No, thank you.

I must find a mouse.

My kittens must have their dinner.

I cannot play all day.

You must play alone."

Alice went to her mother.

She said, "Mother, I came home.

I could not find any playmate.

No one could play all day.

I do not want to play all day.

I will sing Sister to sleep."

Alice sang and sang.

Soon little Sister was fast asleep.

LITTLE BOY BLUE

Little Boy Blue,
Come, blow your horn.
The sheep are in the meadow,
The cows are in the corn.
Where is the little boy
Who looks after the sheep?
He is under the haycock,
Fast asleep.

MOTHER GOOSE

Where are you, Little Boy Blue?

Are you in the house?

Are you in the barn?

Are you in the meadow?

I see you, Little Boy Blue!

You are under the haycock.

Wake up! Wake up!

Blow your horn, Little Boy Blue.
Do you see your sheep?
They are in the meadow.
Where are your cows?
They are in the corn.
Blow your horn, Little Boy Blue!
Take the sheep and the cows
to the barn.

LITTLE BO-PEEP

Little Bo-Peep
Has lost her sheep,
And cannot tell
Where to find them.
Leave them alone,
And they will come home,
And bring their tails
Behind them.

MOTHER GOOSE

Bo-Peep: Good morning, Boy Blue!
I have lost my sheep.

Boy Blue: Have you looked for them?

Bo-Peep: Yes, I have looked for them.

Boy Blue: Did you look in the corn?

Bo-Peep: Yes. They were not there.

Boy Blue: Come with me to the meadow.
We will look for them there.

BOY BLUE: I hear your sheep, Bo-Peep!
I see them, too.

BO-PEEP: Oh, yes! There they are!
They are in the meadow.
I will take them to the barn.

BOY BLUE: I will go with you, Bo-Peep.

BO-PEEP: Thank you, Little Boy Blue.
Bring your horn with you.

BAA, BAA, BLACK SHEEP

Baa, baa, Black Sheep,
Have you any wool?
Yes, sir! Yes, sir!
Three bags full.
One for my master,
One for my dame,
And one for the little boy
Who lives in the lane.

MOTHER GOOSE

GIRL: Good morning, Black Sheep!
Have you any wool?

SHEEP: Yes! I have three bags full.

GIRL: What will you do with it?

SHEEP: One bag is for my master.
One bag is for my dame.
One bag is for Little Boy Blue.

GIRL: Where is Little Boy Blue?

SHEEP: He is in the lane.

SHEEP: Good morning, Boy Blue!
Guess what I have for you.

BOY BLUE: Is it a bag of wool?

SHEEP: Yes, it is a bag of black wool.

BOY BLUE: Thank you, Black Sheep!
Thank you for the wool!
I will take it to mother.
She will make me a coat.
The coat will keep me warm.

THE PIG'S DINNER

Little Pig went down the road.

He wanted some dinner.

Soon he came to a garden.

It was full of pretty flowers.

"Wee, wee!" said Little Pig.

"I want to go into that garden.

Flowers make a good dinner."

He went into the garden.

Soon Red Hen came down the road.

Her little chickens were with her.

By and by they came to the garden.

They saw the pretty flowers.

"Cluck, cluck!" said Red Hen.

"How pretty the flowers are!

Come with me into the garden.

We can find a good dinner there."

They went into the garden to eat.

How happy they all were!

Soon White Cow came down the road.

She saw the pretty flowers.

She saw Little Pig in the garden.

She saw Red Hen and her chickens.

"Moo, moo!" she said.

"How pretty the flowers are!

They will make a good dinner."

Red Hen said, "Cluck, cluck, come in!"

Little Pig said, "Wee, wee, come in!"

White Cow went into the garden.

Soon the farmer came home.

He saw White Cow in the garden.

He saw Red Hen and her chickens.

He saw Little Pig, too.

"Stop eating my flowers!" he said.

"Get out of my garden!"

Away they all ran down the road!

"Good-bye, Mr. Farmer!" said the hen.

"We had a good dinner!" said the pig.

"We will come back soon!" said the cow.

MAUD LINDSAY

PIGGY WIG'S HOUSE

JACK RABBIT: Good morning, Piggy Wig!
Where are you going?

PIGGY WIG: I am going to the woods.
I want to make a house.

JACK RABBIT: May I go with you?

PIGGY WIG: What can you do?

JACK RABBIT: I can cut down trees.
You cannot cut them down.

PIGGY WIG: Come with me. I want you.

GRAY GOOSE: Good morning, Piggy Wig! Where are you going?

PIGGY WIG: I am going to the woods. I want to make a house.

GRAY GOOSE: May I go with you?

PIGGY WIG: What can you do?

GRAY GOOSE: Your house will have cracks. I can fill all the cracks.

PIGGY WIG: Come with me. I want you.

RED COCK: Good morning, Piggy Wig!
Where are you going?

PIGGY WIG: I am going to the woods.
I want to make a house.

RED COCK: May I go with you?

PIGGY WIG: What can you do?

RED COCK: I can wake you up.
I say, "Cock-a-doodle-doo!"

PIGGY WIG: Come with me. I want you.

Soon they came to the woods.

Jack Rabbit cut down the trees.

Piggy Wig made the house.

Gray Goose filled the cracks.

Red Cock woke them up.

"Cock-a-doodle-doo!" he said.

Folk Tale

THE LITTLE PIG

Once there was a little pig.

He lived with his mother in a pen.

One day he saw his four little feet.

"Wee, wee, Mother!" he said.

"See my four little feet!

What can I do with them?"

She said, "You can run with them."

The little pig ran and ran.

He ran round and round the pen.

One day he found his two little eyes.

"Wee, wee, Mother!" he said.

"See my two little eyes!

What can I do with them?"

She said, "You can see with them."

The little pig looked and looked.

He saw his mother.

He saw the cow.

He saw the sheep.

64

One day he found his two little ears.

"Wee, wee, Mother!" he said.

"See my two little ears!

What can I do with them?"

She said, "You can hear with them."

He heard the dog say, "Bow, wow!"

He heard the cat say, "Mew, mew!"

He heard the cow say, "Moo, moo!"

He heard the sheep say, "Baa, baa!"

One day he found his one little nose.

"Wee, wee, Mother!" he said.

"See my one little nose!

What can I do with it?"

She said, "You can smell with it.

Can you smell your dinner?"

The little pig wanted his dinner.

He could not smell it.

"Wee, wee, wee!" he said.

Soon he found his one little mouth.

"Wee, wee, Mother!" he said.

"See my one little mouth!
What can I do with it?"
She said, "You can eat with it.
You can eat your dinner."
The little pig wanted his dinner.
He could not find it.
"Wee, wee, wee!" he said.

Soon a girl came to the pen.

She had something for Piggy.

Can you guess what it was?

The girl said, "Come, Piggy!

Come, Piggy, come!

I have something for you.

It is something good to eat."

What did the little pig hear
with his two little ears?

What did the little pig see
with his two little eyes?

What did the little pig do
with his four little feet?

What did the little pig smell
with his one little nose?

Guess what the little pig did
with his one little mouth.

FOLK TALE

69

LITTLE RABBIT

Stop, stop, Little Rabbit!
Where are you going?
Do not run away from me.
I cannot see you, now.
Where are you, Little Rabbit?
Oh, now I see you!
You are behind the flowers.
You are in the pretty clovers.

Stop, stop, Little Rabbit!

Do not eat the clovers.

They are so pretty.

They are so white.

They are white like your ears.

The clovers are so little, now.

Soon they will be big.

Then you may eat them.

Good-bye, Little Rabbit, good-bye!

L. E. Orth

JACK RABBIT'S VISIT

Father Squirrel lived in a tree.

His home was a hole in the tree.

Mother Squirrel lived there, too.

Three little squirrels lived with them.

They were pretty little squirrels.

They had big eyes and big tails.

They played in the trees.

They played on the ground, too.

One day they were all at home.

They were eating nuts.

Jack Rabbit came along.

He said, "May I come in?"

"Yes, come in," said Father Squirrel.

Jack Rabbit came into the house.

"Sit down," said Mother Squirrel.

He sat down on the floor.

A little squirrel said, "Eat some nuts!"

"No, thank you," said Jack Rabbit.

"I do not like nuts, Little Squirrel."

SQUIRREL: Rabbit, where do you live ?

RABBIT: I live in the ground.
I have a warm hole there.

SQUIRREL: What do you eat?

RABBIT: Oh, I eat leaves.
What do you eat, Squirrel?

SQUIRREL: We eat nuts.
Will you live with us?

RABBIT: No! I cannot live in a tree.
I must go, now. Good-bye!

MARY DENDY

74

BOBBIE SQUIRREL'S TAIL

See Bobbie Squirrel.

What a big tail he has!

One day he ran down a tree.

Jack Rabbit was coming along.

His tail was little.

Jack Rabbit said, "Look at Bobbie!

He wants us to see his big tail."

Brown Owl said, "Oh, see Bobbie!

He has his tail above his back."

Bobbie Squirrel ran to a nut tree.

There were nuts under the tree.

Bobbie made a hole in the ground.

It was a big round hole.

He swept the nuts into it.

He swept them with his big tail.

Bobbie covered them with leaves.

He swept the leaves with his tail, too.

Then he ran to his home in the tree.

He will eat the nuts next winter.

Guess what Bobbie found at home!

He found shells on the floor!

A little squirrel had put them there.

"Oh, dear me!" said Bobbie.

"The floor must be swept!"

So Bobbie swept the floor.

He swept it with his big tail.

By and by, night came.

Bobbie went to sleep on the floor.

Guess what he did with his tail!

Carolyn S. Bailey

NED VISITS GRANDMOTHER

Ned had a little red cart.

He wanted Grandmother to see it.

His mother gave him a big apple.

She gave him some cookies, too.

He put the apple and the cookies
into the cart.

Then he went to see Grandmother.

Soon Ned came to a meadow.

He saw Little Pig there.

"Good morning!" said Ned.

Little Pig said, "Wee, wee!

I want some cookies."

Ned said, "No, no, Little Pig!

They are for Grandmother.

Come with me to her house.

She will give you some dinner."

So Little Pig went along with Ned.

Soon they came to a barn.

Ned saw White Hen.

"Good morning!" said Ned.

White Hen said, "Cluck, cluck!

I want some cookies."

Ned said, "No, no, White Hen!

They are for Grandmother.

Come with us to her house.

She will give you some dinner."

So White Hen went along with them.

Soon they came to a house.

Gray Kitten was in the yard.

"Good morning!" said Ned.

Gray Kitten said, "Mew, mew!

I want some cookies."

Ned said, "No, no, Gray Kitten!

They are for Grandmother.

Come with us to her house.

She will give you some dinner."

So Gray Kitten went along with them.

Soon they came to a big tree.

Little Bird was in the tree.

He flew down to the ground.

"Good morning!" said Ned.

Little Bird said, "Peep, peep!

I want some cookies."

Ned said, "No, no, Little Bird!

They are for Grandmother.

Come with us to her house.

She will give you some dinner."

So Little Bird went along with them.

Grandmother looked down the road.

"What do I see?" she said.

"Oh, it is little Ned!

Good morning, Ned!"

Ned said, "Good morning!

See my red cart, Grandmother!

I have some cookies for you.

I have a big apple for you, too."

Grandmother said, "Thank you, Ned!

I like cookies and apples."

GRANDMOTHER: Ned, what can I give you?

LITTLE NED: Oh, give us some dinner!

GRANDMOTHER: What do you like, Ned?

LITTLE NED: Little Pig likes corn.
White Hen likes corn, too.
Little Bird likes bread.
Gray Kitten likes milk.
I like milk, too.

GANDMOTHER: I will get corn and bread.
I will get milk, too.

Little Bird ate bread.

White Hen and Little Pig ate corn.

Ned and Gray Kitten drank milk.

Grandmother ate the cookies.

She ate the apple, too.

Ned said, "We must go now.

Thank you for the good dinner."

"Good-bye, Ned," said Grandmother.

"Good-bye, Grandmother," said Ned.

Soon they came to the big tree.

"Good-bye, Little Bird," said Ned.

"Peep, peep!" said Little Bird.

Next they came to the house.

"Good-bye, Gray Kitten!" said Ned.

"Mew, mew!" said Gray Kitten.

Next they came to the barn.

"Good-bye, White Hen!" said Ned.

"Cluck, cluck!" said White Hen.

Next they came to the meadow.

"Good-bye, Little Pig!" said Ned.

"Wee, wee!" said Little Pig.

Ned ran to his mother.

MARION WATHEN

NATURE

87

LITTLE OWL

Little Owl lived with Mother Owl.

One night Mother Owl, said, "Whoo!

Big owls say 'Whoo, whoo!'

You must say 'Whoo, whoo.'"

Little Owl said, "Oh, no, Mother!

I don't want to say 'Whoo, whoo.'"

Mother Owl said, "You must say 'Whoo.'

The boy and the cat will hear you.

They will run away from you."

Little Owl would not say "Whoo."

Mother Owl said, "A cat will get you!"

Little Owl said, "What is a cat?"

Mother Owl said, "A cat has big eyes.

It can see at night.

It eats birds."

Little Owl said, "What do cats say?

Do cats say 'Whoo, whoo,' Mother?"

"No, no!" said Mother Owl.

"Cats say 'Mew, mew!'"

"Mother Mother!" said Little Owl.

"I want to see a cat!

I want to hear her say 'Mew, mew!'"

Mother Owl said, "You must say 'Whoo.'

You are not a good little owl."

One day Mother Owl flew away.

Little Owl sat in a tree.

"Mew, mew!" he said. "Mew, mew!"

A cat heard him say, "Mew, mew!"

She said, "Little Owl, Little Owl!

Can you eat a mouse?"

"Oh, yes!" said Little Owl.

The cat said, "Do you eat birds?"

"Oh, no! I am a bird," said Little Owl.

The cat said, "I eat birds.

I will eat you, Little Owl!"

A boy came to the tree.

His name was Bobbie.

He was a kind little boy.

He saw Little Owl and the cat.

Bobbie said, "Cat, go away!

You must not eat Little Owl!

I want to take him home with me.

I want to give him some dinner.

Good-bye, Cat, good-bye!"

So Bobbie took Little Owl home with him.

Little Owl was not happy.

He wanted to go to his mother.

That night Mother Owl came to him.

Little Owl said, "Mother, Mother!

I will be a good little owl.

I will say 'Whoo, whoo!'

Take me home with you."

Mother Owl said, "No, no, Little Owl!

I can not take you with me."

In the morning she flew away.

Little Owl would not eat his dinner.
All day he said, "Whoo, whoo!"
Bobbie's mother heard Little Owl.
She said, "Bobbie, hear Little Owl!
He wants to go to his mother.
Take him to his home."
Bobbie took Little Owl to the woods.
"Mother Owl! Mother Owl!" he said.
"Do you want Little Owl?"
Mother Owl said, "Whoo, whoo!"
Little Owl said, "Whoo, whoo," too.
Bobbie gave Little Owl to his mother.
How happy they all were!

ANNE SCHÜTZE

WHAT BROWN PUSSY SAW

Once Gray Pussy sat in a tree.

Brown Pussy sat on the ground.

Gray Pussy looked at Brown Pussy.

Brown Pussy looked at Gray Pussy.

"Good morning," said Gray Pussy.

"Mew, mew," said Brown Pussy.

"What a pretty coat you have!"

Brown Pussy ran away.

Gray Pussy looked at her.

She said, "See Brown Pussy run!

I wish I could run, too."

Brown Pussy ran to her home.

Guess what she said to her mother!

She said,

"A little gray kitten
   Sat in a tree!
   I looked at her,
   She looked at me!"

KATE L. BROWN

THE BROOK

Brook, brook, come along.
Run along with me!
Oh, what happy playmates
You and I will be!

You can run, I can run.
Both of us can sing,
Tirili, tirili,
Ting, ting, ting!

Brook, brook, come along.
Run along with me!
Oh, dear me, I tumbled in!
What a sight to see!

You are wet, I am wet.
Still we both can sing,
Tirili, tirili,
Ting, ting, ting!

LAURA E. RICHARDS

97

THE WINDMILL

Once there was a big windmill.
It went round and round.
It gave water to the horses and
the cows.
It gave water to the sheep, too.
One day it said, "I will stop!
I will not go round and round."
So the windmill was still all day.

By and by the wind came.

It said, "I will help you, Windmill.

I will make you go round and round and round."

"No, no!" said the windmill.

"I don't want to go round and round and round.

I don't want you to help me.

I want to be still all day."

The wind said, "You must go round!

The horses and cows want water.

I will blow for you."

The windmill would not go.

It would not bring any water.

So the wind went away.

By and by the horses came home.

They had helped the farmer all day.

The cows and the sheep came, too.

They all ran to the windmill.

They all wanted some water.

There was no water for them!

They said, "Oh, Windmill!

Will you be kind to us?

Will you give us water, Windmill?"

The windmill was not happy.

It said, "There is no water.

Wind, come and help me."

The wind came at once.

"I will blow for you," it said.

The windmill went round and round.

Soon the water came.

The horses drank and drank.

The cows and the sheep drank, too.

How happy the windmill was!

KATHLYN LIBBEY

101

WHO LIKES NORTH WIND?

"Oo-oo! Oo-oo!" said North Wind.

Little Bird sat in a tree.

He wanted to keep warm.

"Peep, peep! Peep, peep!" he said.

"How cold the wind is!

Winter is coming.

I must fly away. Good-bye!"

"Oo-oo! Oo-oo!" said North Wind.

Gray Squirrel sat on the ground.

"How cold the wind is!" he said.

"Winter is coming.

There are nuts in the woods.

I will fill my nest with nuts.

I can eat them in the winter.

My nest will keep me warm.

I will go to my home in the tree."

"Oo-oo! Oo-oo!" said North Wind.

Black Kitten was in the yard.

"Mew, mew, mew!" he said.

"How cold the wind is!

Winter is coming.

I want to go into the house.

I can keep warm there.

I can get some milk there, too.

I can sleep on the warm floor.

Mew, mew! Mew, mew!

Let me come into the house!"

"Oo-oo! Oo-oo!" said North Wind.

Jack ran to the barn.

"Hurrah! Hurrah!" he said.

"How cold the wind is!

Winter is coming.

It is going to snow.

I will make a snow man.

I will ride down the hill, too.

Hurrah! Hurrah! Hurrah!"

"Oo-oo ! Oo-oo !" said North Wind.
"How happy I am, now!
I have found a playmate.
Oo-oo, Jack, oo-oo!
The white snow is coming.
See! It is coming now!
You and I will be playmates.
How happy we will be!
Oo-oo, Jack, oo-oo!

FOLK TALE

FESTIVALS

107

HOW PATTY GAVE THANKS

Cow: Good morning to you all!
I have something to tell you.
Can you guess what it is?

Horse: Is it about a little girl?

Cow: Yes! It is about a little girl.
Can you guess who she is ?

Sheep: Is it something about Patty?

Cow: Yes! It is about Patty.

HORSE: I want to hear about Patty.
We all love Patty.

SHEEP: Yes! Tell us about Patty.

COW: What a good girl Patty is!
She came to me this morning.
She said, "Good morning, Cow!
This is Thank You day.
You give me milk.
I like your good milk.
Thank you, Cow, thank you!"
She gave me a big apple.
I like to give milk to Patty.

SHEEP: Bob, did you see Patty?

HORSE: Yes, Patty came to me, too.
She said, "You dear horse!
You give me rides.
Thank you, Bob, thank you!"
She patted me and patted me.
Then she gave me some hay.
I will give her a ride soon.

COW: How kind Patty is!
Bob likes to give her rides.
I like to give her milk.

HORSE: Did Patty thank you, Sheep?

SHEEP: Yes, she came to us, too.
She said, "Good morning!
I know what you give me.
You give me wool.
The wool keeps me warm.
Thank you, thank you!"
Then she gave us some water.

COW: How kind Patty is!
Bob likes to give her rides.
Sheep like to give her wool.
I like to give her milk.

Cow: Did Patty thank the hens, too?

Horse: Yes! I heard her thank them.
Then she gave them some corn.

Sheep: What do the hens give Patty?

Cow: They give her eggs.

Horse: She said "Thank you" to us all.

Cow: How kind Patty is!
Bob likes to give her rides.
Sheep like to give her wool.
Hens like to give her eggs.
I like to give her milk.

EMILIE POULSSON

THE LITTLE CHRISTMAS TREE

Once there were three trees.

They lived on a hill.

One tree was big.

One tree was not so big.

One tree was little.

The snow came down upon them.

They said, "Christmas is coming!

We want to be Christmas trees!"

A little bird came along.

The little bird was lost.

He could not find his mother.

He went to the big tree.

"Are you a kind tree?" he said.

"May I sit in your branches?

The snow is so cold!"

The big tree said, "No, no!

I don't want birds in my branches.

I am going to be a Christmas tree!"

"How cold I am!" said the bird.
"I wish I could find a kind tree!
It would keep me warm."
He went on up the hill.
Soon he came to the next tree.
"Are you a kind tree?" he said.
"May I sit in your branches?
The snow is so cold!
I am lost, dear Tree.
I can not find my mother."
Now the tree was not kind.
It was like the big tree.
It said, "No, Little Bird, no!
I don't want birds in my branches.
I am going to be a Christmas tree!"

"How cold I am!" said the bird.

"I wish I could find a kind tree!"

He went on up the hill.

Soon he came to the little tree.

He said, "Little Tree, I am lost!

May I sit in your warm branches?

The snow is so cold!"

Now the little tree was kind.

It was not like the other trees.

It said, "Oh, yes, dear Bird!

You may sit in my branches."

How happy the little bird was!

116

By and by the bird heard something.

A sleigh was coming up the hill!

It did not stop at the big tree.

It did not stop at the next tree.

On it went to the little tree.

"It has come to us!" said the bird.

A man jumped out of the sleigh.

Can you guess who he was?

"What a pretty tree!" said the man.
"I want it for a Christmas tree."
So he took it with him in the sleigh.
He took the little bird, too.
He said, "I will take you to Patty.
She will keep you warm."
Away they all flew in the sleigh.
How happy the little tree was!
How happy the little bird was!

MARY McDOWELL

OUR FLAG

I know three little sisters.
You know the sisters, too.
For one is red, and one is white,
The other one is blue.

Hurrah for the three little sisters!
Hurrah for the red, white, and blue.
Hurrah! Hurrah! Hurrah! Hurrah!
Hurrah for the red, white, and blue.

E. L. McCord

THE EASTER RABBIT

Little Rabbit sat by the road.

Ray and May came along.

They did not see Little Rabbit.

"Easter is coming soon," said May.

"Let us make a nest in the yard.

The Easter Rabbit will see it.

He will leave pretty eggs in it for us."

Ray said, "Yes, let us make a nest!"

Away they ran to make the nest.

Little Rabbit ran to his mother.

"I want to be the Easter Rabbit," he said.

"What is the Easter Rabbit?" said his mother.

"The Easter Rabbit puts eggs into nests," he said.

"Ray and May are going to make a nest in the yard.

I want to put eggs into it."

His mother said, "Do not go away! Ray and May will get you."

Mother Rabbit went to the garden.

Then Little Rabbit ran away.

He wanted to find Easter eggs.

Ray and May saw Little Rabbit.

They ran after him.

"Stop, Little Rabbit!" said Ray.

"Stop! We want you.

Oh, now we have you!

We will keep you in the barn."

They took Little Rabbit to the barn.

They patted him and patted him.

They gave him leaves for dinner.

Little Rabbit wanted his mother.

Ray said, "The rabbit is not happy.

Let us take him to the yard.

He will put Easter eggs into the nest!"

They took Little Rabbit to the yard.

Away he ran down the road!

By and by Little Rabbit stopped.

He said, "I will go back to the yard.

I want to make Ray and May happy.

I want to be the Easter Rabbit.

I will look for eggs in the yard."

Little Rabbit ran back to the yard.
He could not find any eggs there.
Then he looked in the nest.
Can you guess what he saw?
He saw two little kittens!
One kitten was white.
The other kitten was black.
Then he saw the mother cat.
She had a gray kitten in her mouth.
She put it into the nest, too.

Soon May came to the nest.

She was looking for Easter eggs.

"Oh, see the kittens!" she said.

"Come, Ray! See what is in the nest!"

Ray ran to look in the nest.

"What pretty kittens!" he said.

How happy Ray and May were!

Little Rabbit was happy, too.

"The cat is the Easter Rabbit!" he said.

Then he ran home to his mother.

ANNE SCHÜTZE

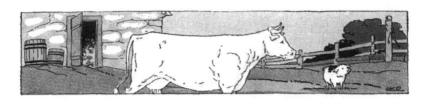

IN THE BARNYARD

Once there was a big barnyard.

White Cow and Piggy Wig lived in it.

Red Hen and Gray Pony lived there, too.

Piggy Wig said, "Wee, wee!

What a good day to eat and sleep!"

Red Hen said, "Cluck, cluck!

What a good day to go to the garden!"

White Cow, said, "Moo, moo!

What a good day to eat hay!"

Gray Pony said, "Good morning!

What a good day to give rides!"

Piggy Wig said, "Wee, wee!
I want to eat and sleep.
I don't want to give rides."
Red Hen said, "Cluck, cluck!
I want to go to the garden.
I don't want to give rides."
White Cow said, "Moo, moo!
I want to go to the meadow.
I want to eat hay there.
I don't want to give rides."
Gray Pony said, "I want to run.
I want to give master a ride."

The master came to the barnyard.

He said, "Piggy Wig, eat your dinner.

You may eat and sleep all day.

Red Hen, go to the garden.

You will find something to eat there.

White Cow, go to the meadow.

You will find hay there.

Gray Pony, come to me.

We will go to see a sick girl.

She lives far, far away."

The master jumped upon Gray Pony.

Away they went galloping, galloping, galloping.

By and by they came to the home of the sick girl.

The master went into the house.

Soon he came back to Gray Pony.

He said, "We helped the sick girl.

She can go out to play, soon.

You are a good pony."

How happy Gray Pony was!

The master jumped upon Gray Pony.

He said, "Now we will go home."

Away they went galloping back to the barnyard.

Red Hen said, "Cluck, cluck, Gray Pony!
I ate corn in the garden."
White Cow said, "Moo, moo!
What a good day I have had!
I ate hay in the meadow."
Piggy Wig said, "Wee, wee!
What a good sleep I have had!
I had a good dinner, too."
Gray Pony said, "How happy I am!
I have had a good day, too.
I helped the little girl."

FRANCES WELD DANIELSON

SLUMBERLAND

131

ALICE AND THE BIRD

Alice was fast asleep.

A bird saw her.

"Wake up! Wake up!" sang the bird.

"Wake up, Little Girl!" it sang.

Alice woke up!

She jumped out of her bed.

She saw the bird in the tree.

Alice went to play with Patty.

She took her doll with her.

Patty said, "I want the doll!"

Alice said, "No, I want it!"

"Give up! Give up!" sang the bird.

Alice looked up into the tree.

There sat the bird!

"Give up! Give up!" it sang.

"I hear you, Little Bird," said Alice.

"I will give up! I will give up!

Patty, you may have the doll."

Alice went home to dinner.

Her mother was not there.

"Oh, where is mother?" she said.

"I want my dinner!"

"Cheer up! Cheer up!" sang the bird.

Alice looked up into the tree.

There sat the bird!

"Cheer up! Cheer up!" it sang.

"I will cheer up," said Alice.

"I will cheer up and be happy."

She ran to play with her kitten.

She sang and was happy.

After dinner, Alice went for a ride.

Then her mother put her to bed.

Her black eyes would not shut.

"Shut them up!" sang the bird.

"Shut them up! Shut them up!"

"I will shut them up," said Alice.

Soon she was fast asleep.

How happy the bird was!

It had helped Alice all the day.

EMILY ROSE BURT

DARK PONY

Once there was a pony.
His name was Dark.
He took boys and girls to Sleepytown.
One night a boy stopped him.
The boy's name was Noddy.
Noddy said,
        "Take me down
        To Sleepytown!"
Noddy jumped upon Dark Pony.
    Away they went galloping, galloping,
galloping.

Soon they came to a little girl.

The girl's name was Niddy.

Niddy said,

"Let me go, too,

Take me with you!"

Dark Pony stopped galloping.

Noddy said, "We will take you."

Niddy jumped up behind Noddy.

"Go, go, Dark Pony!" she said.

Away they went galloping, galloping, galloping.

137

Soon they came to a white dog.

The dog said,

"Bow, wow, wow!

Take me now!"

Dark Pony stopped galloping.

Noddy jumped down to get the dog.

Then he jumped upon the pony.

"Go, go, Dark Pony!" he said.

Away they went galloping, galloping, galloping.

Soon they came to a black cat.
The cat said,

"Mew, mew, mew!

Take me, too!"

Dark Pony stopped galloping.

Niddy jumped down to get the cat.

Then she jumped upon the pony.

She took the cat with her.

"Go, go, Dark Pony!" she said.

Away they went galloping, galloping, galloping.

By and by they came to a barn.

They saw a red cock there.

The red cock said,

"Cock-a-doodle-doo!

Take me, too!"

Dark Pony stopped galloping.

Niddy said, "Come, Red Cock!

You may sit behind me."

The red cock flew up behind Niddy.

"Go, go, Dark Pony!" said Niddy.

Away they went galloping, galloping, galloping.

Soon they came to the woods.

They saw a gray squirrel there.

The squirrel said,

>"Take me, too,
>
>Along with you!"

Niddy said, "Yes, Gray Squirrel.

We will take you.

Sit by the red cock."

The squirrel sat by the red cock.

"Go, go, Dark Pony!" said Niddy.

Away they went galloping, galloping, galloping.

They went galloping on and on.

How happy they all were!

They sang and sang and sang.

By and by Dark Pony stopped.

He had come to Sleepytown.

All the eyes were shut.

Niddy and Noddy and White Dog and Black Cat and Red Cock and Gray Squirrel were all fast asleep.

THE ALPHABET

a   b   c   d   e   f   g   h
i   j   k   l   m   n   o   p   q   r
s   t   u   v   w   x   y   z

A   B   C   D   E   F   G   H
I   J   K   L   M   N   O   P   Q   R
S   T   U   V   W   X   Y   Z

WORD LIST

The following list contains the words used in the *Primer* that have been developed in the *Pre-Primer* work. The number indicates the page on which the word first appears.

a, 9

and, 13

are, 15

away, 10

baa, 24

barn, 11

bird, 10

bow-wow, 33

boys, 23

can, 16

cat, 9

cluck, 26

coo, 23

cow, 23

dinner, 9

do, 29

dog, 17

dove, 29

eggs, 20

father, 16

find, 9

flew, 10

fly, 22

garden, 55

gave, 12

girls, 19

give, 23

go, 30

good-bye, 22

hen, 26

house, 12

I, 13

in, 16

is, 13

it, 10

like, 13

little, 17

may, 36

me, 13

mew, 15

milk, 12

moo, 23

mother, 20

mouse, 11

nest, 19

no, 9

not, 17

one, 14

play, 28

rabbit, 62

rained, 15

ran, 11

run, 63

said, 9

sat, 20

saw, 10

see, 14

she, 18

sheep, 24

some, 18

the, 9

them, 12

they, 15

three, 20

to, 9

tree, 19

two, 19

we, 9

wet, 15

white, 13

will 9

yes, 17

you, 16

145

The following list contains the words in the *Primer* that were not taught in the *Pre-Primer* lessons. A number of these words have been developed phonetically in earlier lessons and are therefore not new to the child when read on the pages indicated. Such words are printed in italic type.

9 Alice	22 soon	apples	45 playmate
come	could	31 *he*	fast
10 kittens	23 wings	any	asleep
too	don't	morning	46 blow
11 went	wish	have	*horn*
12 for	had	32 who	under
13 Spot	want	tell	haycock
my	24 wool	33 thank	47 *wake*
black	keeps	34 farmer	up
14 has	warm	35 with	49 Bo-Peep
four	25 horse	36 bag	lost
gray	rides	full	tails
15 day	27 all	37 did	behind
was	happy	bring	51 hear
were	am	38 sing	52 sir
sleep	28 where	sister	dame
16 basket	Mr. *Jay*	meadow	lives
what	*land*	39 must	lane
guess	of	make	54 coat
18 her	that	master	55 pig
19 pretty	far	40 leave	down
20 on	29 Mrs.	alone	road
from	love	41 corn	came
blue	*how*	your	flowers
21 there	get	42 oh	*wee*
after	above	take	56 red
sang	30 Bobbie	43 home	chickens
looked	his	44 their	by